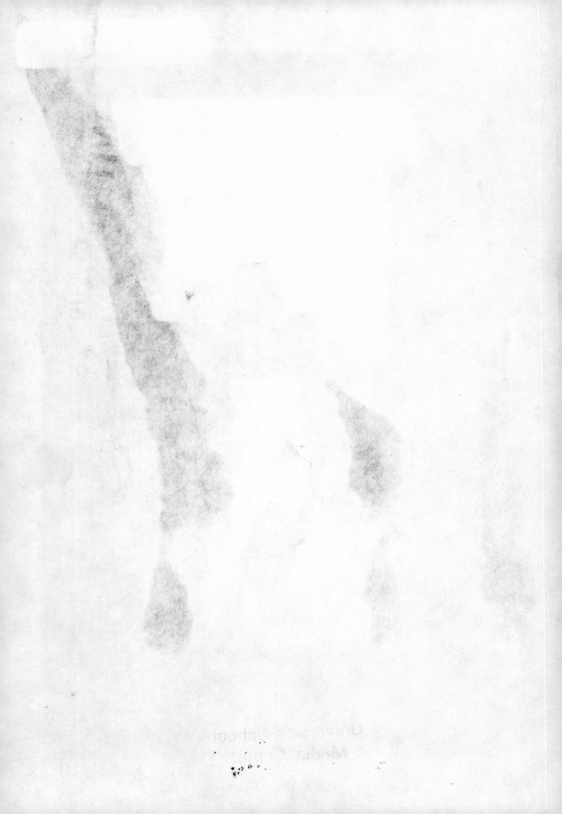

Pig's New Hat

Pig's New Hat

By Ethel and Leonard Kessler
Pictures by Pat Paris

GARRARD PUBLISHING COMPANY
CHAMPAIGN, ILLINOIS

For Kim, who loves new hats

Library of Congress Cataloging in Publication Data

Kessler, Ethel.
    Pig's new hat.

    (Begin to read with Duck and Pig)
    SUMMARY: Pig's new hat is the cause of much
admiration and excitement during an outing in the park.
    [1. Hats—Fiction. 2. Animals—Fiction] I. Kes-
sler, Leonard P., 1920-   joint author. II. Paris,
Pat. III. Title.
PZ7.K483Pi   [E]   80-17373
ISBN 0-8116-7551-3

Pig's New Hat

"Duck and I
are going to the park,"
said Pig.
"I will put on my new hat."

On the way they met Frog.
"What a pretty hat,"
said Frog.

"Thank you, Frog.
What a pretty tie,"
said Pig.

"Let's sit here,"
said Duck.
"I'm hungry.
Let's eat," said Pig.

University School
Media Center

"That was good,"
said Pig.
"I'm sleepy,"
said Duck.

"I will pick
pretty flowers
for my new hat,"
said Pig.

Pig ran under the fence
and across the field.

"What pretty flowers!"
said Pig.
"I will pick some.

Go away, Bee," said Pig.
"Go away!"

Pig ran across the field
and under the fence.
The bee buzzed
around Pig's hat.

"Help! Help!"
Pig cried.

Pig hit Duck
with her hat.

"Sorry, Duck,"
said Pig.
"It did not hurt,"
said Duck.
"Let's go out
in the boat.

Pig, you sit here,"
said Duck.

"Look," said Pig.
"What pretty flowers.
I will pick some
for my hat."

"Sit down, Pig,"
said Duck.
"You can't swim!"

The boat turned over.
Pig and Duck fell
into the water.

"Help! Help!
I can't swim,"
cried Pig.

"I will help you,"
said Duck.
And Duck did.

"What is the matter?"
said Duck.
"I lost my hat,"
cried Pig.
"Let's go home."

On the way home,
they met Frog.

"Did you catch some fish?"
said Duck.
"No fish," said Frog.
"But look!"

"It's my hat,"
cried Pig.
"But the flowers are gone."

"Here is a pretty tie for you,"
said Frog.
Frog put it
around Pig's hat.

30

Pig put on her hat.

"Thank you," said Pig.

"It's pretty," said Duck.

"But it needs some flowers."

"No," said Pig.
"No flowers!
It's pretty
just the way it is."